SUE'S
SKY
Story by
LULU BUCK
Illustrations by
CHRYS ZYX
Photography by
TRISTAN OWEN

FriesenPress

Suite 300 - 990 Fort St
Victoria, BC, V8V 3K2
Canada

www.friesenpress.com

First Edition — 2020

Illustrated by Chrys Zyx

Photography by Tristan Owen

ISBN
978-1-03-911842-3 (Hardcover)
978-1-03-911841-6 (Paperback)
978-1-03-911843-0 (eBook)

1. *Juvenile Fiction, Diversity & Multicultural*

Distributed to the trade by The Ingram Book Company

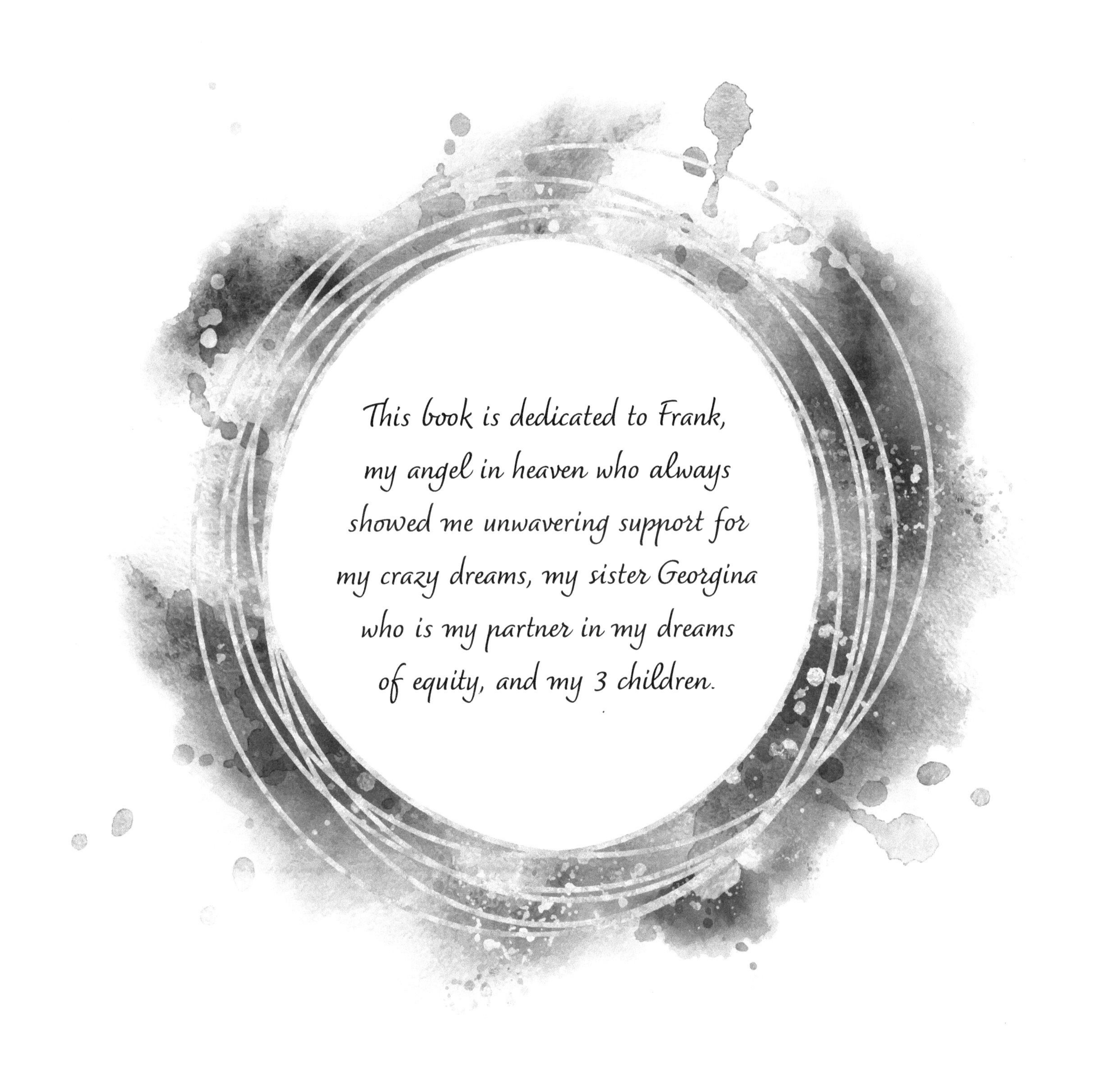

*This book is dedicated to Frank,
my angel in heaven who always
showed me unwavering support for
my crazy dreams, my sister Georgina
who is my partner in my dreams
of equity, and my 3 children.*

One day,
Sue was walking to school.
On her way she looked up in
the sky and said to herself,
"Wow! The blue sky is
very beautiful today."

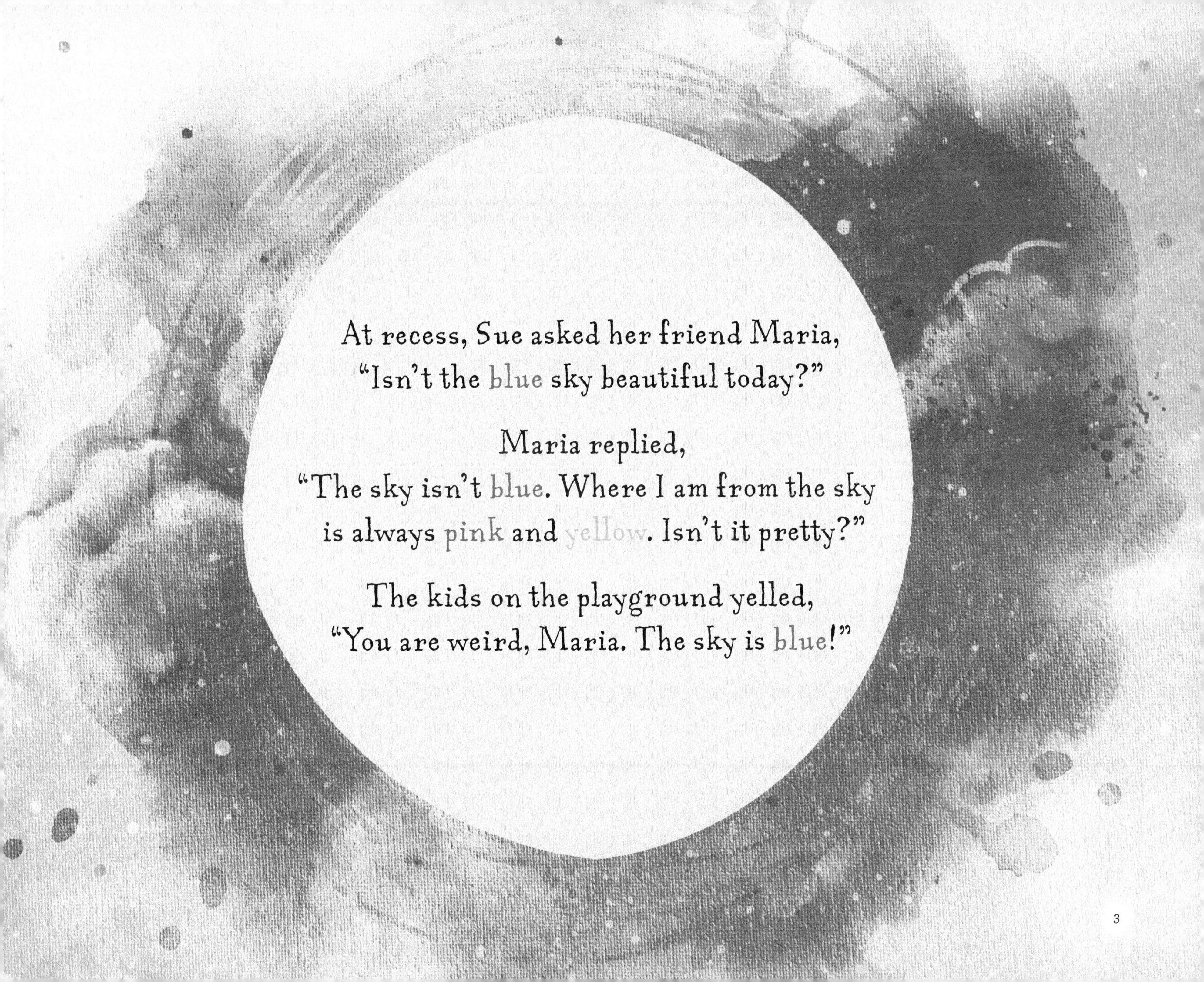

At recess, Sue asked her friend Maria,
"Isn't the blue sky beautiful today?"

Maria replied,
"The sky isn't blue. Where I am from the sky is always pink and yellow. Isn't it pretty?"

The kids on the playground yelled,
"You are weird, Maria. The sky is blue!"

Sue quickly replied,
"She isn't weird! I think it is neat that
Maria sees the sky as pink and yellow
and, **THAT'S OK**."

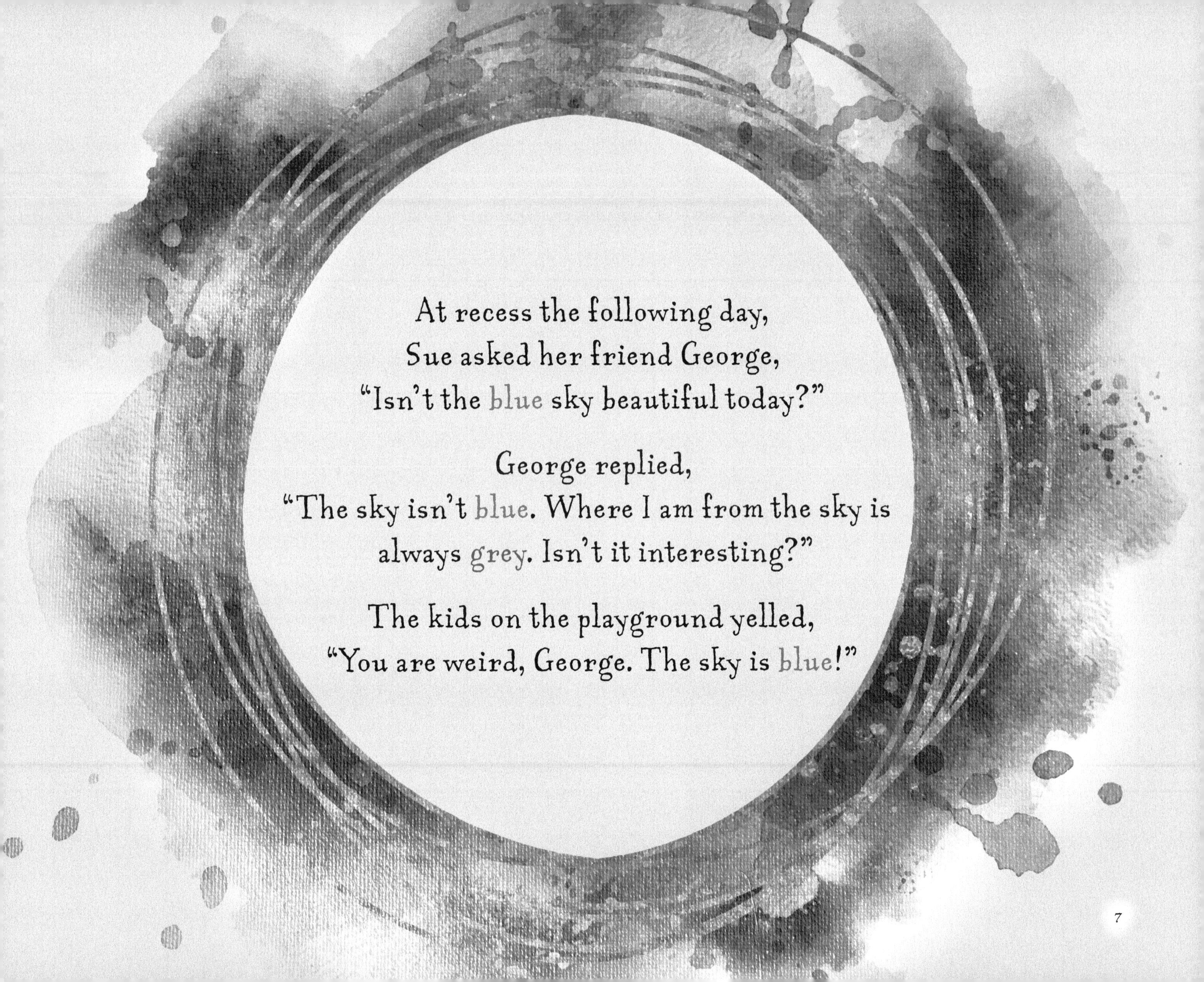

At recess the following day,
Sue asked her friend George,
"Isn't the blue sky beautiful today?"

George replied,
"The sky isn't blue. Where I am from the sky is always grey. Isn't it interesting?"

The kids on the playground yelled,
"You are weird, George. The sky is blue!"

Sue quickly replied,
"He isn't weird! I think it is neat that
George sees the sky as grey,
and **THAT'S OK.**"

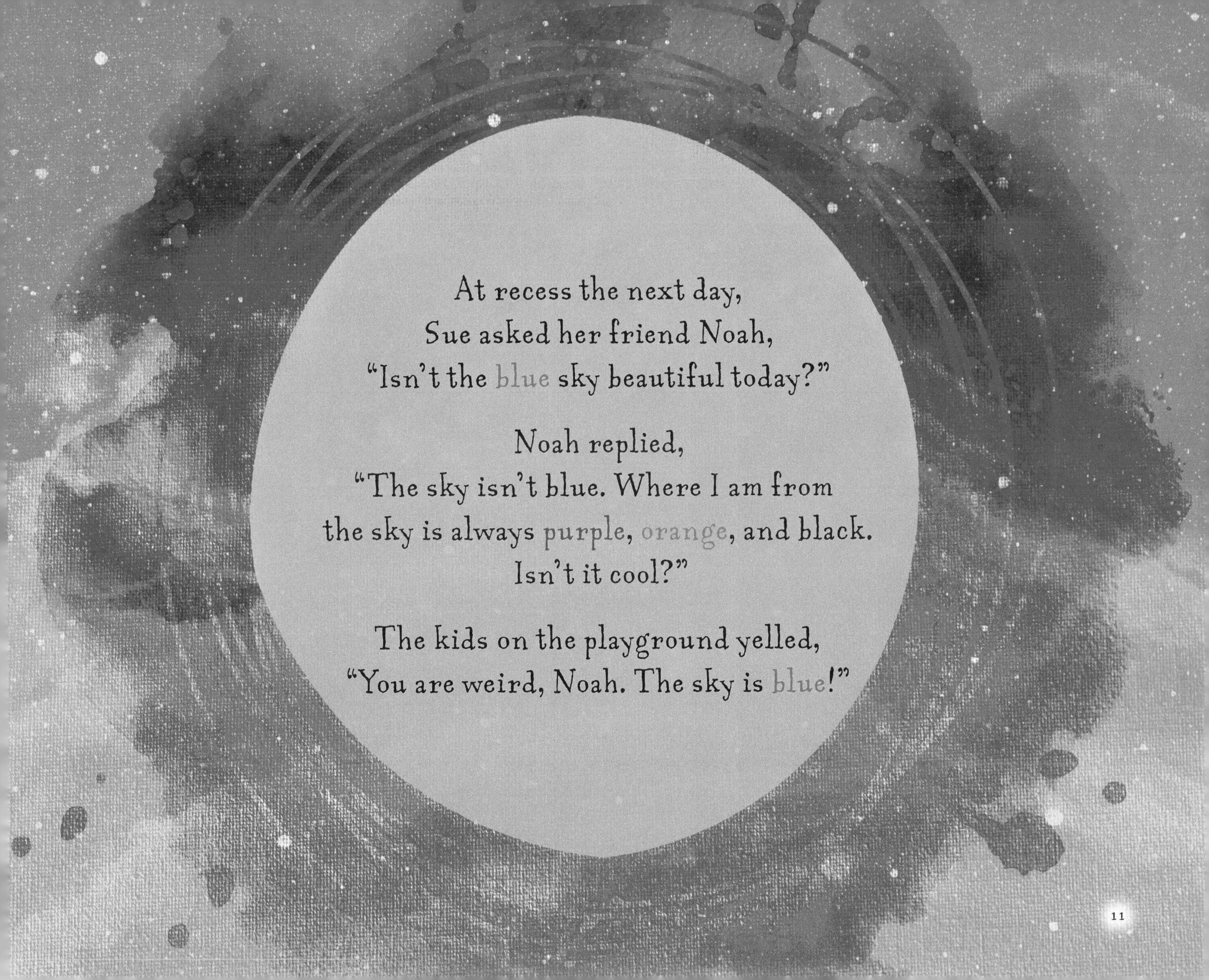

At recess the next day,
Sue asked her friend Noah,
"Isn't the blue sky beautiful today?"

Noah replied,
"The sky isn't blue. Where I am from
the sky is always purple, orange, and black.
Isn't it cool?"

The kids on the playground yelled,
"You are weird, Noah. The sky is blue!"

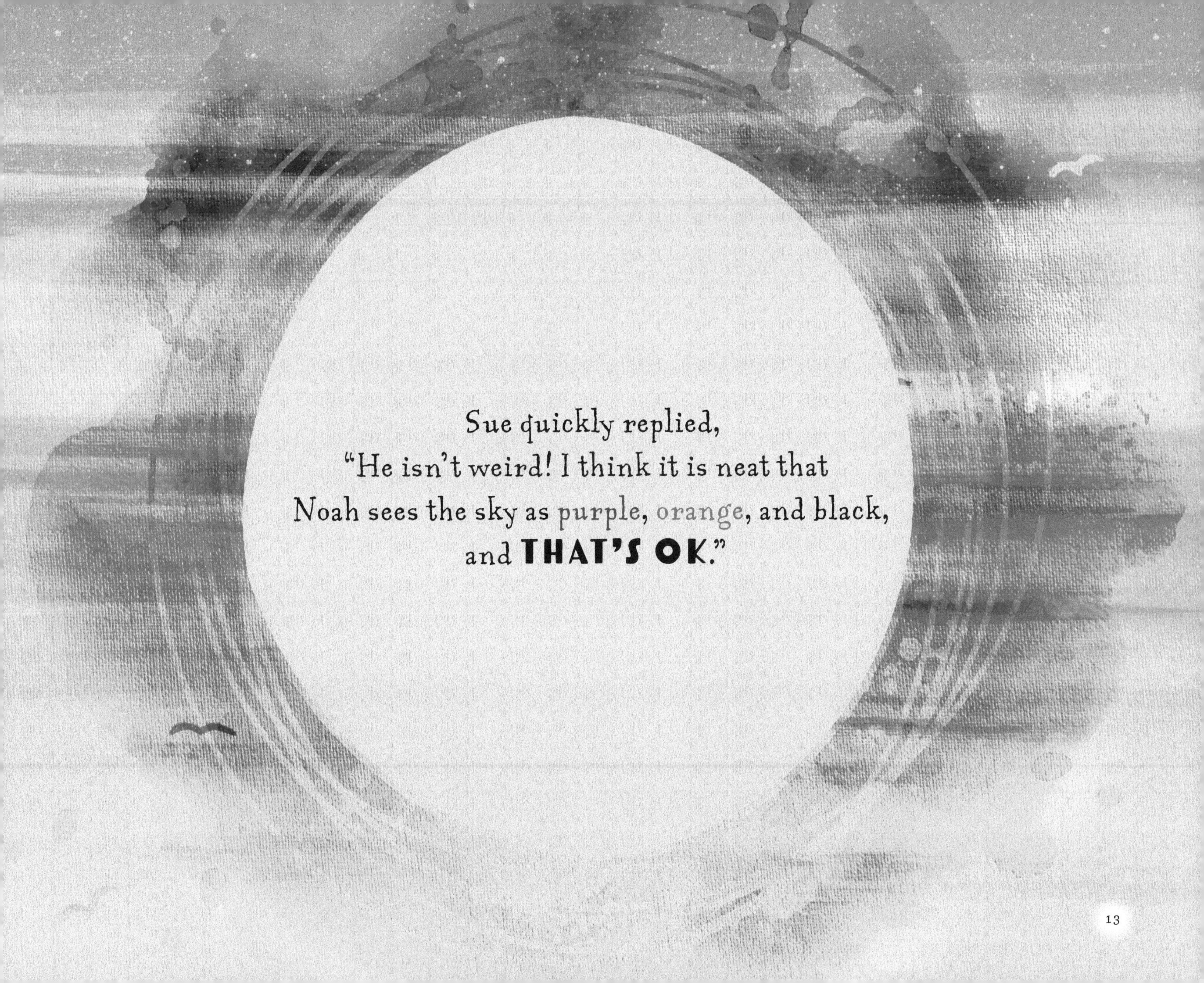

Sue quickly replied,
"He isn't weird! I think it is neat that
Noah sees the sky as purple, orange, and black,
and **THAT'S OK**."

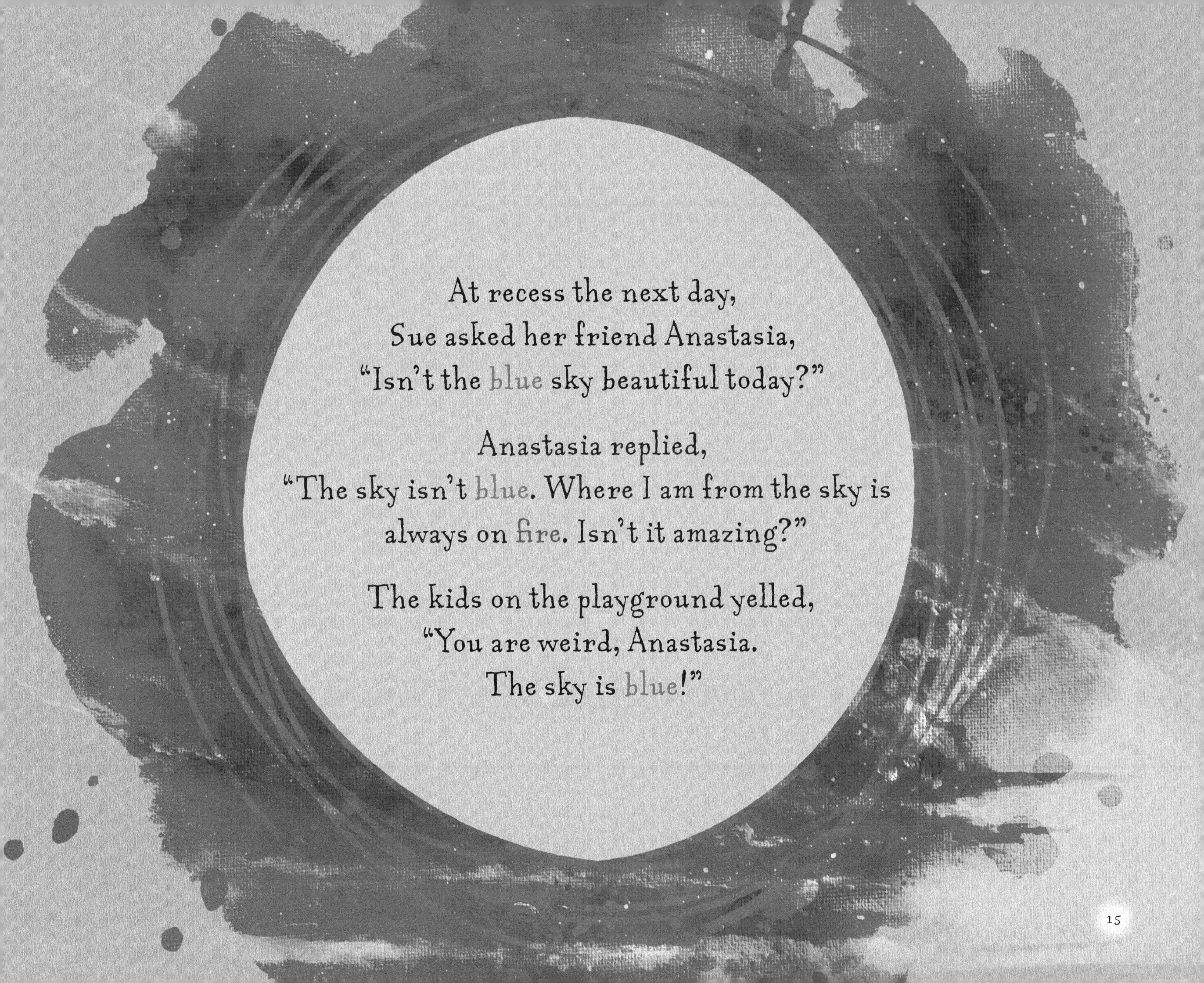

At recess the next day,
Sue asked her friend Anastasia,
"Isn't the blue sky beautiful today?"

Anastasia replied,
"The sky isn't blue. Where I am from the sky is always on fire. Isn't it amazing?"

The kids on the playground yelled,
"You are weird, Anastasia.
The sky is blue!"

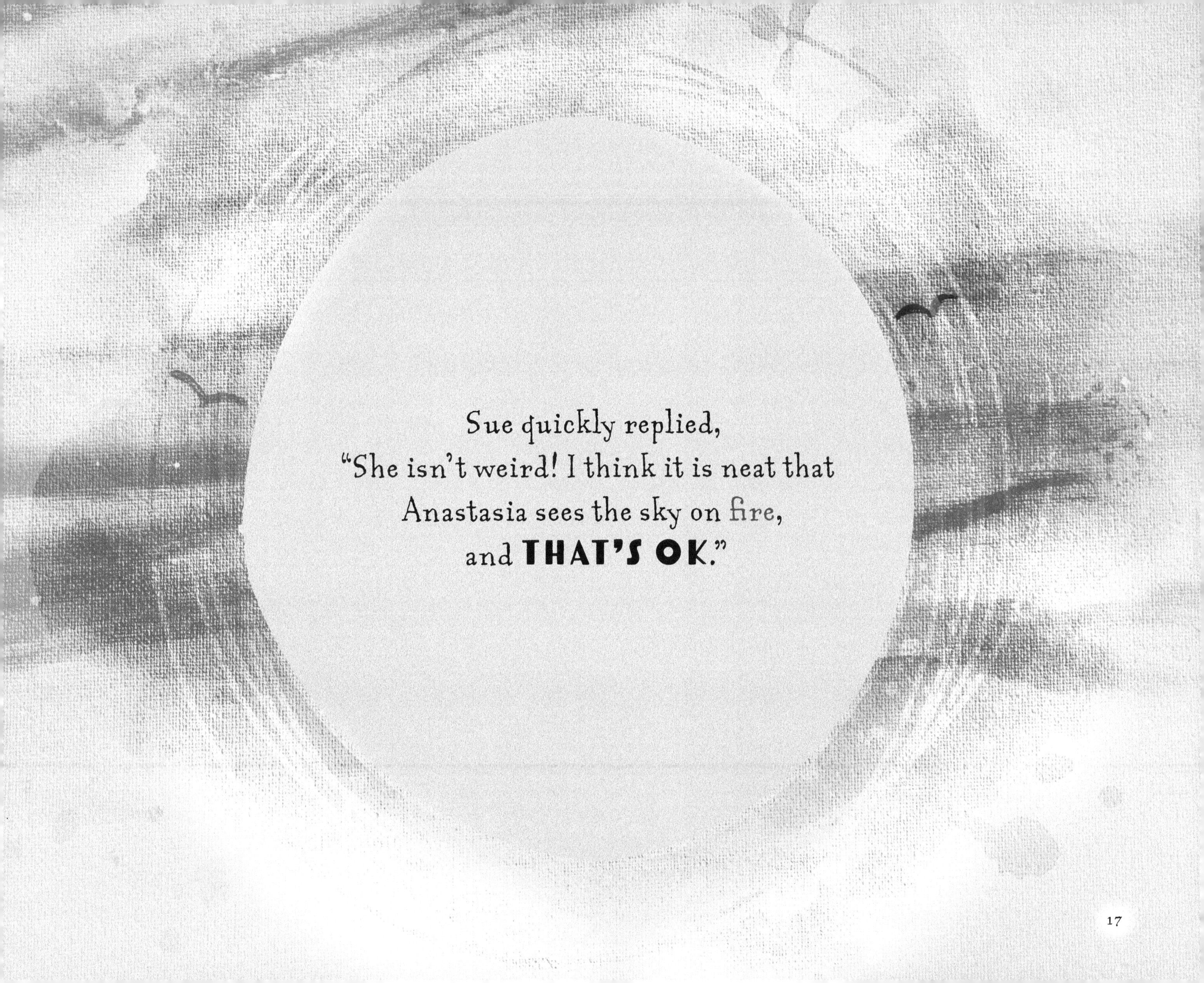

Sue quickly replied,
"She isn't weird! I think it is neat that
Anastasia sees the sky on fire,
and **THAT'S OK**."

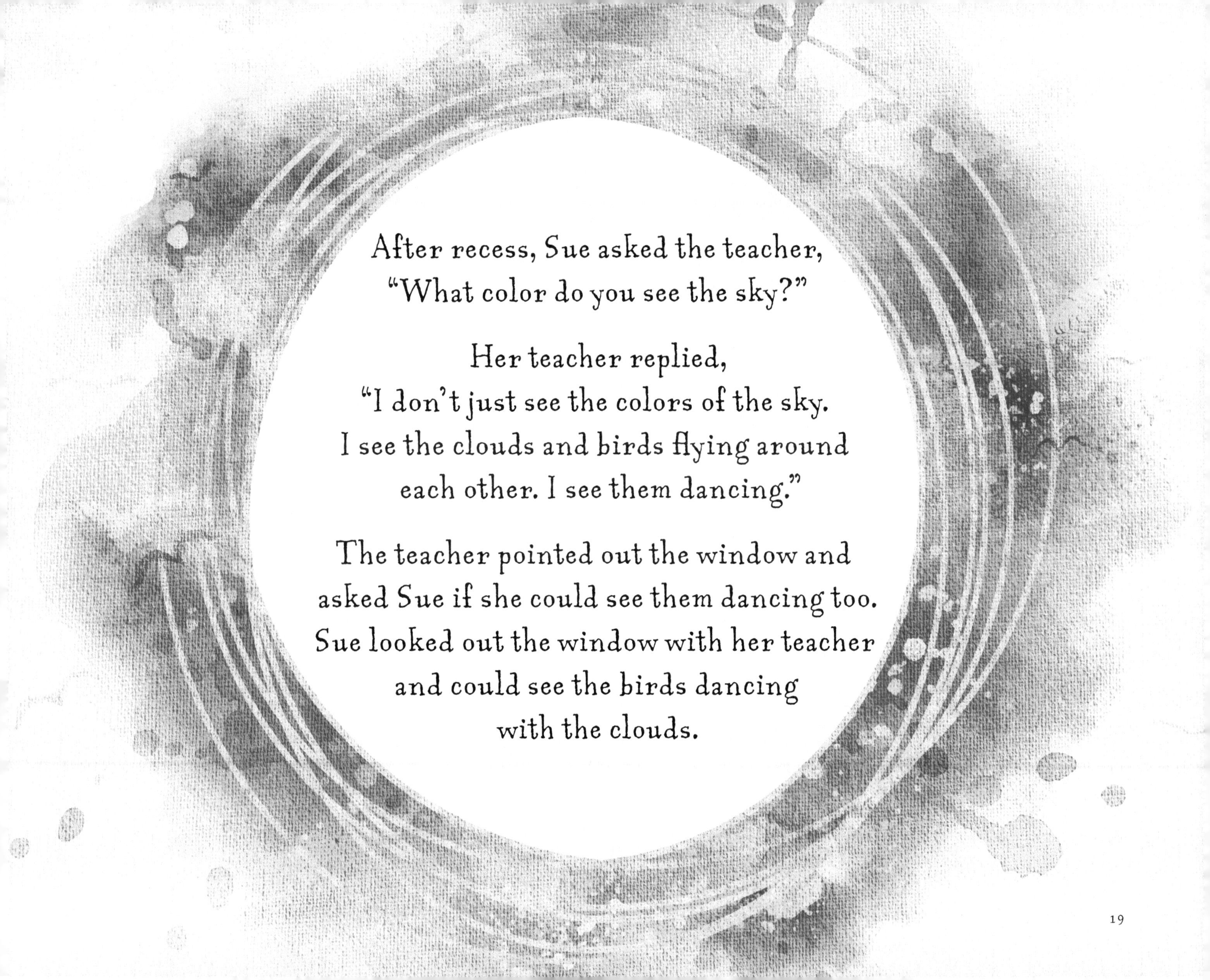

After recess, Sue asked the teacher,
"What color do you see the sky?"

Her teacher replied,
"I don't just see the colors of the sky.
I see the clouds and birds flying around
each other. I see them dancing."

The teacher pointed out the window and
asked Sue if she could see them dancing too.
Sue looked out the window with her teacher
and could see the birds dancing
with the clouds.

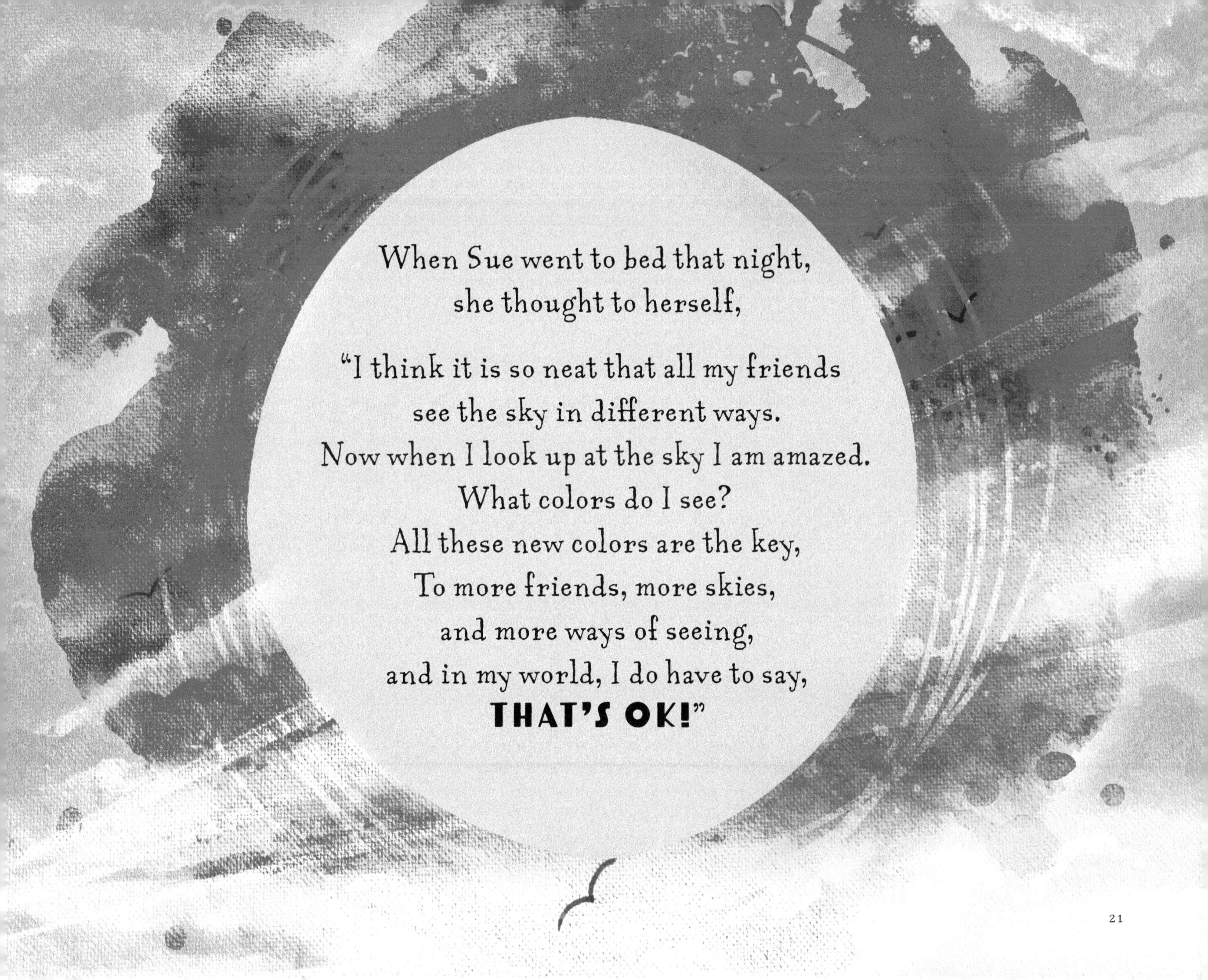

When Sue went to bed that night,
she thought to herself,

"I think it is so neat that all my friends
see the sky in different ways.
Now when I look up at the sky I am amazed.
What colors do I see?
All these new colors are the key,
To more friends, more skies,
and more ways of seeing,
and in my world, I do have to say,
THAT'S OK!"

Lulu Buck has been a public educator for twenty-three years and is currently the Coordinator of Educational Equity and Family Engagement for St Vrain Valley schools.

Previously, Lulu was an English Language Development and World Language Senior Consultant for the Office of Culturally and Linguistically Diverse Education, and the Standards and Instructional Support Office at the Colorado Department of Education. She was also the CDE's Coordinator for the Colorado Seal of Biliteracy for High School Diplomas and Dual Language Education. Lulu was most passionate about her role as a state trainer for cultural responsiveness and equity for districts and schools, through which she had the honor of training thirty-eight Colorado school districts. She also taught English and Spanish for ten years in public secondary schools.

In 2009, she was awarded Teacher of the Year through the Colorado Congress for Foreign Language Teachers, and most recently "A Friend of the Profession" by SWCOLT. *Sue's Sky* is her first book. She lives in Colorado with her two sons and their dogs.

CPSIA information can be obtained
at www.ICGtesting.com
Printed in the USA
BVHW062208260622
640642BV00001B/2

9781039118416